Published by
Louis Weber, C.E.O.
Publications International, Ltd.
7373 North Cicero Avenue
Lincolnwood, Illinois 60712

Ground Floor, 59 Gloucester Place
London W1U 8JJ

Customer Service: 1-800-595-8484 or customer_service@pilbooks.com

www.pilbooks.com

p i kids is a registered trademark of Publications International, Ltd.

8 7 6 5 4 3 2 1

ISBN-13: 978-1-4127-3491-2
ISBN-10: 1-4127-3491-6

A Child's Garden of Blessings

Written by
Virginia Ragland Biles

Illustrated by
Tiphanie Beeke, Rob Hefferan, Maranda Maberry,
Robin Moro, David Wojtowycz, Jennifer Fitchwell, Christopher Moroney

pi
kids ®   publications international, ltd.

Good Morning, God

Good morning, God. I am here
To say thank you loud and clear.
Thank you for the morning light.
Thank you for the sunshine bright.
Thank you for the grass so green.
Thank you for the birds that sing.
Thank you for the rain that falls,
Like your love, it covers all.

Morning Prayer

Thank you, God, for another day.
Guide my steps along the way
And show me now the things to do
To make my life a joy to you.

Sunshine

The sun peeked in my window,
And I went outside to play.
I frolicked in its golden rays
All the livelong day.

When the sunshine said goodbye
And night began to come,
I said, "Please hurry back,"
To my good friend the sun.

Breakfast

Here are my bowl and cup.
My spoon just fits my hand.
I whisper a prayer to God
That he will understand.

Please bless my bowl of cereal.
Please bless this little girl, too.
Guide my steps and playtime.
Keep me safe the whole day through.

Getting Ready

I'm ready, I'm ready,
I'm ready to go.
School starts tomorrow,
And I want you to know:
I'm ready to write,
And I'm ready to read.
I have new shoes and a backpack
Filled with things that I need.
I have crayons and a ruler
And pencils that erase,
But, most of all,
I've got a huge smile on my face!

The Wrong Side of the Bed

I get up on the wrong side of the bed.
I stomp my foot and shake my head.
When Mommy tells me what to do,
I'm ugly, I frown, and I am rude.

I stick out my tongue, I hit my sister.
Mommy says to me, "Listen, Mister.
I don't like how you're acting today.
God doesn't want you to behave this way."

So I go back to bed and get up again.
I know that God is listening in
To everything I do and say.
He doesn't want me to act this way.

I get up again with a smile on my face.
I sit at the table and say my grace.
All day long, I'm as good as can be
'Cause I love God, and God loves me.

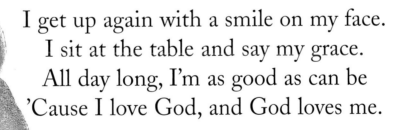

Sharing

I shared my blocks with Bobby.
I shared my truck with Jim.
But I didn't share my blankie
With either one of them.

I shared my cookie with Jean.
I let Joanie play with my farm.
But I kept my soft blue blankie
Safe within my arms.

Teacher said it's time to nap.
God wants me to go to sleep.
So she covered me with my blankie
From my head down to my feet.

My blankie gave me happy dreams.
It kept me safe and warm.
My blankie is like God's great love.
I slept in God's soft blue arms.

Hopscotch

One.
Two.
Three.
God loves me.
Six.
Seven. Eight.
God is great!
Hop. Hop.
Hop.
Back I go.
Hop.
Hop.
Hop.
Time to throw!

Questions and Answers

Who made me?
Did the same God who made me
Make the ferocious lion and the little bumblebee?

Yes, indeed!
The same God who gave you
That sweet smile and eyes of blue
Gave the bumblebee his stinger, too.

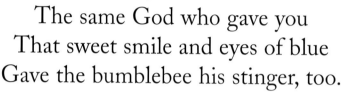

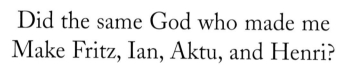

Did the same God who made me
Make Fritz, Ian, Aktu, and Henri?

Yes, indeed!
The same God who made you
made them red, black, and yellow, too.

Does God know their names?
Does he love us all the same?

Yes, indeed!
God knows each child.
He knows your name and where you dwell.
He knows and loves you all so well.

Perseverance

Anna bit me yesterday,
And I said, "That's not nice!"
I tried to be her friend,
But then she bit me — twice!

I know some day she'll play with me;
Some day she'll be my friend.
So now I turn the other cheek;
I'm hopeful till the end.

Going to School

I love to go to school!
I love to write and read.
I study hard and try to learn
The secrets to succeed.

Rainbow

I saw a rainbow today,
God's colors in the sky,
A promise to mankind that
The world would never die.

My Prayers Float
Like Clouds

My prayers float up
Like white clouds in the sky.
God's hands gather them in;
Then he sends his reply.
God's answers come down
Like cooling drops of rain.
Flowers begin to bloom
And all is right again.

Seasons

Thank you, God, for summer,
For the sun's hot rays, the buzz of the bee,
For the gurgling creek,
And the shade of the maple tree.

Thank you, God, for fall,
For the red and gold trees that line the roads,
For the geese flying south,
And long walks in the woods.

Thank you, God, for winter,
For warm woolen mittens, winds that chill,
For snow that makes drifts,
And sleds that zoom down the hill.

But most of all, thank you, God, for spring,
For the fields filled with flowers,
And the earth turned green
Through God's perfect power.

Grandma's Stories

When I go to visit Grandma,
I'm as happy as I can be.
First I give her a real big hug,
Then I sit upon her knee.

She tells me tales of days gone by
When Dad was only three.
She reads me stories she used to read
When another boy sat on her knee.

Our family Bible holds the best
Of all the ones she reads.
I curl up in her lap and wait
To hear about their deeds.

I like to hear about young boys
Who lived so long ago.
Stories of boys who'd be the kind
Of friends I'd like to know.

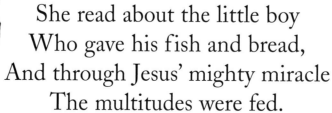

She read about the little boy
Who gave his fish and bread,
And through Jesus' mighty miracle
The multitudes were fed.

Samuel heard the Lord call out
His name so loud and clear.
"Samuel, Samuel," the Lord said,
"Samuel, please, come here."

She read about Moses in the bulrushes,
Who was saved from cruel slaughter.
His mother gave her own dear son
To live with Pharaoh's daughter.

Moses was a special boy.
He was a special man.
With God's guidance he did lead
His people to the promised land.

But Jesus is my favorite boy
In all Grandma's Bible stories.
She tells me how he was born to men
To save us all for glory.

I like to hear about these boys;
They were so small like me.
And long ago each may have sat
Upon his grandma's knee.

My Baby Sister

When Mommy brought the new baby home,
I thought she was so sweet.
She had soft hair and sleepy eyes
And two little tiny feet.

I held her bottle and patted her back.
I held her in my arms.
I whispered "I love you" in her ear
And "Where did you come from?"

Mommy heard me talking to her.
"She's a gift from God," she said.
"He knew you needed a sister, dear,
Someone to sleep in your old bed."

I'm glad I have a sister now.
I can hardly wait to play.
God sent me a little friend,
And I thank him every day.

Grandpa Got Sick

Grandpa got really sick last year.
He couldn't play with us at all.
He couldn't play ride the horsie
Or toss the rubber ball.

All day long he sat in his chair
While we played around his feet.
Grandma said "Not so loud" to us.
So we whispered our messages sweet.

God looked down and heard our prayers.
He listened to tales we had to tell.
He gave his blessings to dear Grandpa
And Grandpa slowly got well.

Helping Mommy

I tie her apron around my middle.
It's too big for me, or I am too little.
But I mop and sweep as I am able,
I set the places on our table—
A fork, a plate, a glass, and a mug.
Mommy says thanks and gives me a hug.
And that is my reward!

I Have Lots of Friends

I have lots of friends
Who are always there for me.
I see them every Sunday,
They're my church family!

Picnic

We're going on a picnic,
Grandma and Grandpa, too.
We've chicken, eggs, and sandwiches.
Enough for me and you!

We'll spread out our blanket
Underneath the tree.
We'll have such fun—
Just you wait and see!

We'll play in the creek,
We'll look for stones,
We'll make some s'mores
And then go home.

Moving Away

Suzuki left our school today.
She moved to a country far away.
We were sad to see her go,
And we wrote her notes to tell her so.

"Goodbye, Suzuki," my note said,
"And tonight when I go to bed
I'll say a special prayer for you,
Your brother, your sister, your parents, too."

God, look after my good friend Sue,
Her brother, her sister, her parents, too.
Keep them safe within your hand
As they travel to a far-off land
And make their home in a new country,
And bring her back to visit me.

Best Friends

Melissa is my best friend.
She lives next door to me.
We play together every day.
We are happy as can be.

Some days we ride our bikes around.
Some days we dress our dolls.
We put them in their fancy hats
And take them for a stroll.

We go to Sunday School together.
We go to church to pray.
We stand up for each other
And promise to be best friends always.

Mealtime Blessing

Thank you for my blue bowl.
Thank you for this food.
Help me do your will today,
And help me to be good.
Lord Jesus, come our guest to be
And bless this food bestowed by thee.

In God We Trust

My nickel says
"In God We Trust,"
And I trust him every day.
Because of him
I have food to eat
And a garden
In which to play.

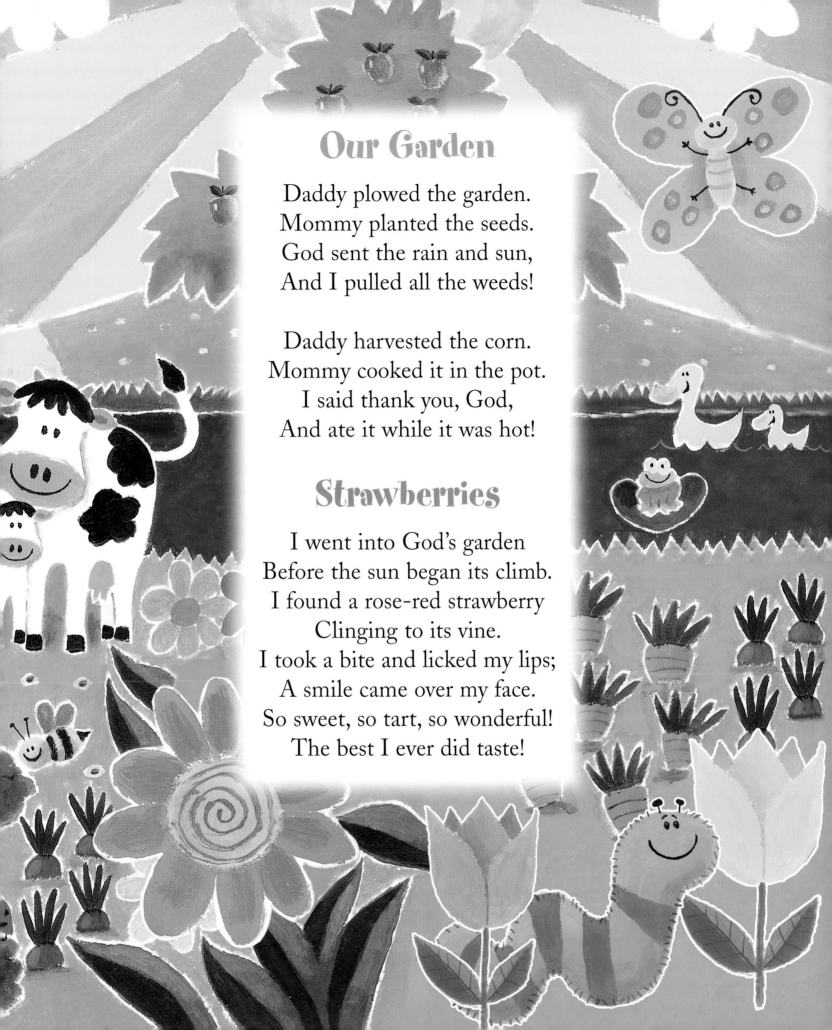

Our Garden

Daddy plowed the garden.
Mommy planted the seeds.
God sent the rain and sun,
And I pulled all the weeds!

Daddy harvested the corn.
Mommy cooked it in the pot.
I said thank you, God,
And ate it while it was hot!

Strawberries

I went into God's garden
Before the sun began its climb.
I found a rose-red strawberry
Clinging to its vine.
I took a bite and licked my lips;
A smile came over my face.
So sweet, so tart, so wonderful!
The best I ever did taste!

The Night Jesus Was Born

The night Jesus was born
Oh, how the heavens rang!
"Hallelujah! Hallelujah!"
God's own angels sang.

The night Jesus was born
A star shone in the sky.
It led the lowly shepherds
To Mary's sweet lullaby.

What Can I Do?

What can I do to bring peace on earth?
I'm just a little child.
How can I tell the Savior's birth?
I'm just a little child.

I can tell the story sweet
About Jesus, gentle and mild,
To everyone I know and meet.
I am a little child!

When Jesus Was a Boy

When Jesus was a little boy like me,
Did he fly a kite, have a toy, climb a tree?
Did he push his sister?
Throw blocks at his brother?
Disobey his father?
Stick out his tongue at his mother?
Was he good as good can be?
Or was he a normal boy like me?

Some Days

Some days I feel
Like it's winter in my soul.
That's when I remember
That I've been told
I'm my own best friend.
So I smile and hug myself,
And it's summer once again.

Happy Birthday, Jesus

Happy Birthday, dear Jesus,
In a stable you were born.
Happy Birthday, dear little baby.
Only swaddling cloths to keep you warm.

The animals looked on
When you were born long ago.
Your mother sang you lullabies
In tones so sweet and low.

No birthday cakes were baked for you,
No icing for you to taste.
No flickering candles to blow out
To mark your special day.

Today we bake a cake for you,
Make it chocolate through and through.
We light the candles and we sing,
"Happy Birthday, Jesus, to you!"

Easter

We go to church on Sunday,
My whole family.
I pray a very special prayer
For Jesus, who died for me.

He was a perfect man,
This savior of mine,
And God took him to heaven
To live with him, Jesus divine.

Celebrations

Fourth of July,
Way up high.
Silvery celebrations,
Fireworks in the sky!

Fifth of July,
Way up high.
Perfect exhilaration,
God's stars in the sky.

Day's End

I've said my prayers,
I've kissed my mom.
I have my teddy
In my arms.

Before I go to bed,
I just want to say,
Thank you, Lord,
For a perfect day!

Going to Bed

I have bubbles in my bath
And toys in my tub.
I have crackers for my snack
And chocolate milk in my cup.

I have warm footie 'jamas
And a blankie so warm,
A story read by Daddy
Resting safely in his arms.

Then it's off to my bed
And turn off my light,
A prayer to sweet Jesus
To keep me safe through the night.

Dream

Candy and cookies,
Sunshiny weather,
Lions and lambs
Playing together.

Fluffy white bunnies,
Popsicles and ice cream,
Rainbows and daisies
All dance in my dream.

Blessing

Bless this house.
Keep it safe from fire and storm.
Bless this family
And keep it snug and warm.

Good Night

Give me my blankie.
Tuck me in tight.
Give me a drink of water.
Now turn off the light.

I'm ready to go to sleep.
I put my thoughts away.
I close my eyes tonight
To open them at day.

God will watch me
While I quietly sleep.
He will guide my dreams
And watch over me keep.

LIGHTNING
BOLT
BOOKS™

All Charged Up

A Look at Electricity

Jennifer Boothroyd

Lerner Publications Company
Minneapolis

To Girl Scout troop 10067, whose energy is quite shocking!

Lerner Publications Company
A division of Lerner Publishing Group, Inc.
241 First Avenue North
Minneapolis, MN 55401 U.S.A.

Website address: www.lernerbooks.com

Library of Congress Cataloging-in-Publication Data

Boothroyd, Jennifer, 1972–
    All charged up : a look at electricity / by Jennifer Boothroyd.
        p.   cm. — (Lightning bolt books™—Exploring physical science)
    Includes index.
    ISBN 978–0–7613–6094–0 (lib. bdg. : alk. paper)
    1. Electricity—Juvenile literature. I. Title.
    QC527.2.B665 2011
    537—dc22   2010027981

Manufactured in the United States of America
1 — CG — 12/31/10

Contents

What Is Electricity?

Electricity is a form of energy. Many people depend on electricity.

Electricity brings light to the library so that this girl can read.

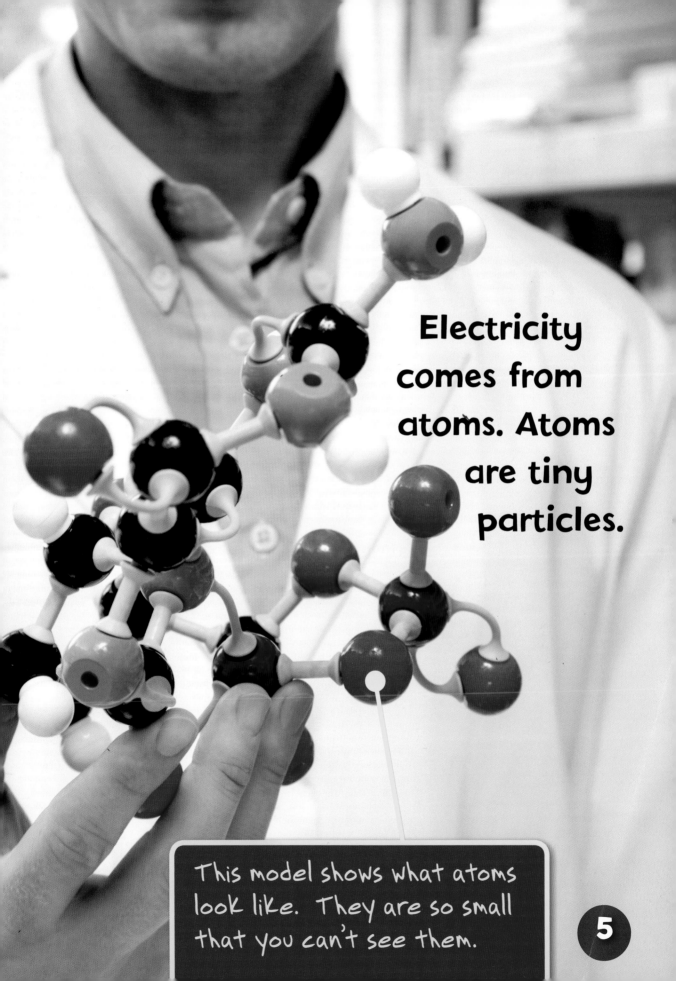

Electricity comes from atoms. Atoms are tiny particles.

This model shows what atoms look like. They are so small that you can't see them.

Everything on Earth is made of atoms. Books, desks, air, and even you are made of atoms!

Atoms have three parts.
Protons and neutrons are in
the center. Electrons circle
around the center.

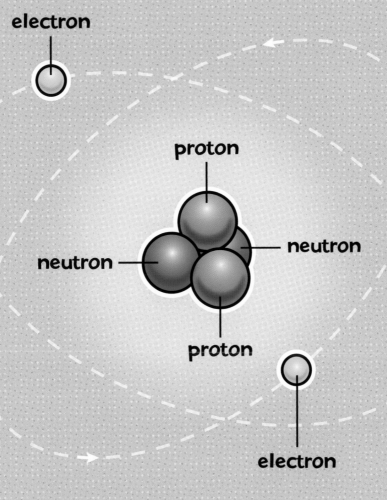

electron

proton

neutron

neutron

proton

electron

The Parts of an Atom

Electrons moving between atoms make electricity.

Electricity is created when electrons travel from one atom to another.

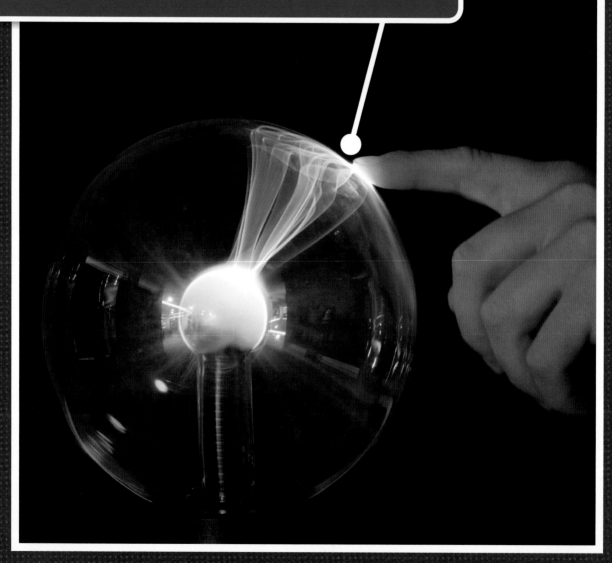

Static Electricity

Static electricity is made when two objects rub together. You can see and feel static electricity. It makes your hair stand up.

Has your hair ever stood on end after you combed it? The comb rubbing against your hair makes electrons move between atoms.

9

Static electricity can make sparks. Some sparks are tiny.

You may see tiny sparks when a sweater rubs against you as you put it on.

Other sparks are huge.
Lightning is a huge spark of
static electricity.

Lightning is made
when ice crystals
rub together inside
a cloud.

Current Electricity

Static electricity lasts for only a short time.

When a comb stops rubbing on your hair, electrons stop moving between atoms. Your hair will soon lie flat.

Electricity lasts longer when there's a steady flow of electrons. A steady flow of electrons is called an electric current.

An electric current makes this lantern glow.

An electric current flows through a conductor. A conductor is any material that lets electrons move from atom to atom. Copper is a great conductor.

Copper wires do a good job of carrying electric current.

Wood and rubber are not good conductors. Electricity does not move through them easily.

The soles of sneakers are made of rubber. Electricity does not travel well through rubber.

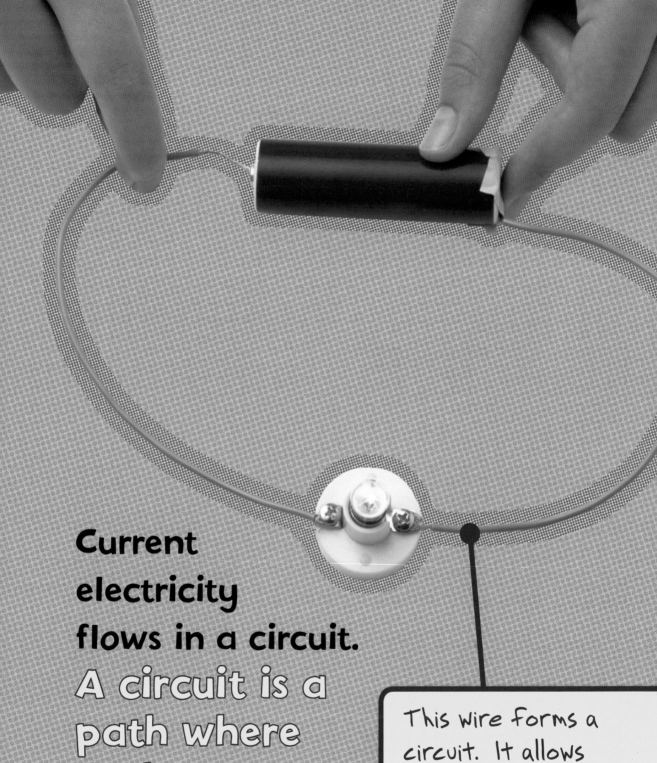

Current electricity flows in a circuit.

A circuit is a path where both ends are connected.

This wire forms a circuit. It allows the current of electricity to light up the lightbulb.

A switch can stop and start the flow of electricity. Flip the switch to turn on the lights. Push the power button to turn off the TV.

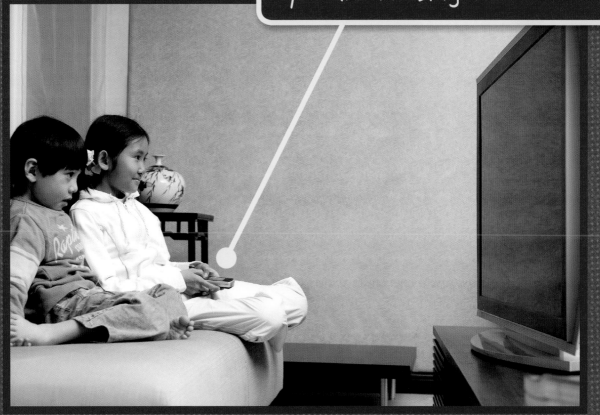

Use electricity wisely. Turn off TVs and lights when you aren't using them.

Sources of Electricity

Current electricity is created at power plants. Power plants are factories that make electricity.

This is a power plant.

Some power plants use water to make electricity. Others burn coal. Still others use energy from the sun or the wind.

Machines called turbines turn wind energy into electricity.

The electricity from power plants travels through wires. The wires carry electricity into buildings. People plug power cords into outlets to use the electricity.

Power wires such as these carry electricity into homes.

Batteries are also sources of electricity.

Batteries store electricity. They let people use electricity without wires from a power plant.

Cars have a large battery.
The electricity from the battery
helps cars
start.

A watch has
a small battery.
The battery gives
the watch power.

People must be careful with electricity. Electricity can burn your skin. It can cause a fire.

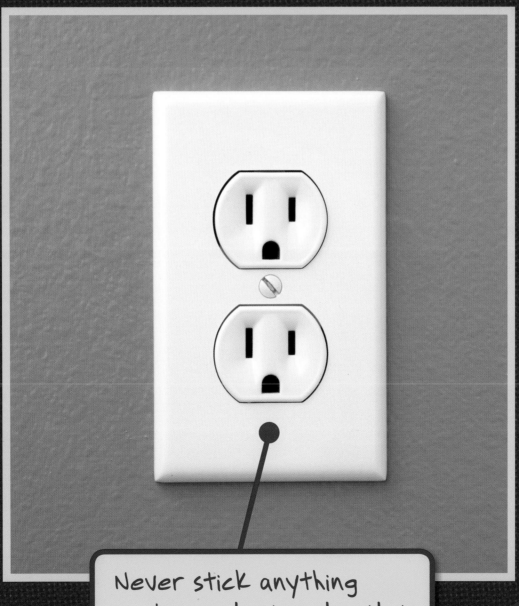

Never stick anything inside an electrical outlet.

Uses for Electricity

Many people use electricity every day. Electricity can make heat.

The heat from an electric stove cooks food.

Electricity can make light and sound.

Electricity powers the equipment that lets you watch a movie.

Electricity can put things into motion.

Electricity helps these clothes dryers run.

19

Electricity is an important part of our lives.

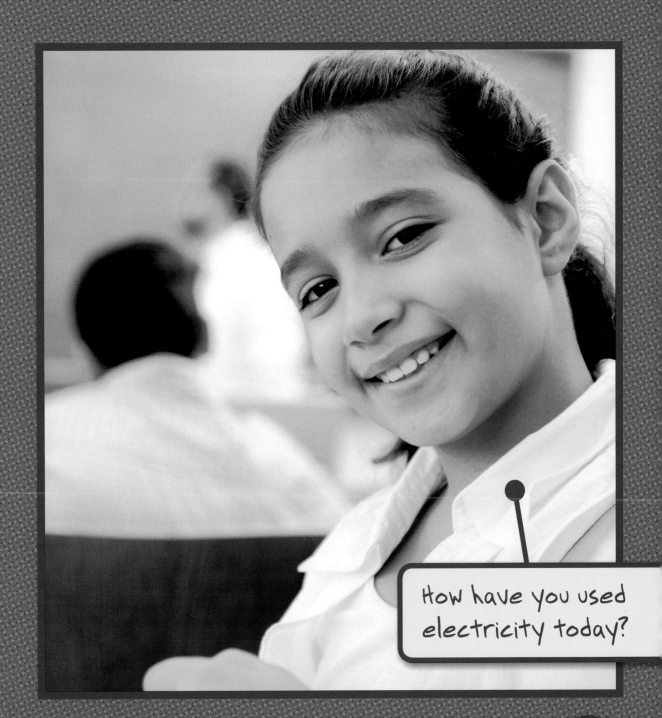

How have you used electricity today?

Activity
Static Sorter

Static electricity can be used to sort tiny objects quickly. Try this activity to see how it works.

What you need:

a pinch of sugar

a pinch of black pepper

a plastic comb

a piece of wool fabric

What you do:

1. Make a small pile of sugar and pepper on a counter. The sugar and pepper should be mixed together.

2. Rub the comb with the wool fabric very quickly for thirty seconds. The comb is now charged with static electricity.

3. Hold the comb a few inches over the pile. Slowly lower the comb over the pile.

4. Stop when the pepper starts sticking to the comb. The pepper sticks first because it is lighter than the sugar.

Glossary

atom: a tiny particle. Everything on Earth is made of atoms.

circuit: a path where both ends are connected

conductor: any material that allows electrons to keep moving from atom to atom

electric current: a steady flow of electrons between atoms

electron: one of the three parts of an atom. Electrons circle around an atom's center.

neutron: one of the three parts of an atom. Neutrons are in the center of an atom.

power plant: a large factory that makes electricity

proton: one of the three parts of an atom. Protons are in the center of an atom.

static electricity: a kind of electricity made when two objects rub together

Further Reading

The Bakken Museum
http://www.thebakken.org

BBC Schools Science Clips:
Using Electricity
http://www.bbc.co.uk/schools/
scienceclips/ages/6_7/electricity.shtml

Frankenstein's Lightning Laboratory
http://www.miamisci.org/af/sln/frankenstein/
safety.html

Schuh, Mari C. *Electricity*. Minneapolis: Bellwether Media, 2008.

Walker, Sally M. *Electricity*. Minneapolis: Lerner Publications Company, 2006.

Waring, Geoff. *Oscar and the Bird: A Book about Electricity*. Cambridge, MA: Candlewick Press, 2009.

Index

Photo Acknowledgments

The images in this book are used with the permission of: © Ronen/Shutterstock Images, p. 2; © Dave& Les Jacobs/Blend Images/Getty Images, p. 4; © Glow Wellness/ SuperStock, p. 5; © Monkey Business Images/Dreamstime.com, p. 6; © Laura Westlund/ Independent Picture Service, p. 7; © Heinrich van den Berg/Gallo Images/Getty Images, p. 8; © iStockphoto.com/Heidi Anglesey, p. 9; © Laurence Monneret/The Image Bank/Getty Images, p. 10; © iStockphoto.com/Paul Lampard, p. 11; © Andersson, Staffan/Johner Images/Getty Images, p. 12; © Radius Images/Photolibrary, p. 13; © iStockphoto.com/syagci, p. 14; © iStockphoto.com/Spencer Sternberg, p. 15; © Dave King/Dorling Kindersley/Getty Images, p. 16; © Corbis/Photolibrary, p. 17; © Harrison Shull/Aurora/Getty Images, p. 18; © Jon Boyes/Photographer's Choice RF/Getty Images, p. 19; © Ted Foxx/Alamy, p. 20; © Karyn R. Millet/Workbook Stock/Getty Images, p. 21; © iStockphoto.com/hywit dimyadl, p. 22 (top); © David Good/Shutterstock Images, p. 22 (bottom); © iStockphoto.com/Patrick Herrera, p. 23; © Photoboxer/Dreamstime.com, p. 24; © Stockbyte/Getty Images, p. 25; © Caroline Schiff/Blend Images/Getty Images, p. 26; © Zurijeta/Shutterstock Images, p. 27; © Tyler Boyes/Shutterstock Images, p. 28 (wool scarf); © justin maresch/Shutterstock Images, p. 28 (black pepper); © EuToch/ Shutterstock Images, p. 28 (blue comb); © Jzzzzs/Dreamstime.com, p. 28 (sugar); © 350jb | Dreamstime.com, p. 30; © carroteater | Dreamstime.com, p. 31.

Front cover: © David R. Frazier Photolibrary Inc./Alamy.